The Crazy Christmas Angel Mystery

Beverly Lewis

THE CUL-DE-SAC KIDS

Katie and Jake and the Haircut Mistake

www.BeverlyLewis.com

THE CUL-DE-SAC KIDS

The Crazy Christmas Angel Mystery

Beverly Lewis

BETHANY HOUSE PUBLISHERS
MINNEAPOLIS, MINNESOTA 55438

© 1993 by Beverly Lewis

Bethany House Publishers edition published 1995. Originally published by Star Song Publishing Group under the same title.

Published by Bethany House Publishers
11400 Hampshire Avenue South
Bloomington, Minnesota 55438
www.bethanyhouse.com

Bethany House Publishers is a division of
Baker Publishing Group, Grand Rapids, Michigan

Printed in the United States of America by
Bethany Press International, Bloomington, MN

ISBN 978-1-55661-627-3

                    Library of Congress Cataloging-in-Publication Data
Lewis, Beverly.
     The crazy Christmas angel mystery / Beverly Lewis
           p.   cm.—(The cul-de-sac kids ; 3)
     Summary: Eric wants to find out about the old man who has
moved in next door, so he and the other Cul-de-sac Kids decide to
pay him a Christmas visit.
     ISBN 1-55661-627-9 (pbk.)
     [1. Christmas—Fiction. 2. Old age—Fiction.
3. Neighborliness—Fiction. 4. Christian life—Fiction.] I. Title.
II. Series: Lewis, Beverly. Cul-de-sac kids. ; 3.
PZ7.L58464Cr   1994
[Fic]—dc20   97-49118

Interior illustrations by Barbara Birch

15   16   17   18   19   20   21   31   30   29   28   27   26   25

To

MARY ERICKSON

Your cheerful heart
and gentle words
make me smile.

THE CUL-DE-SAC KIDS

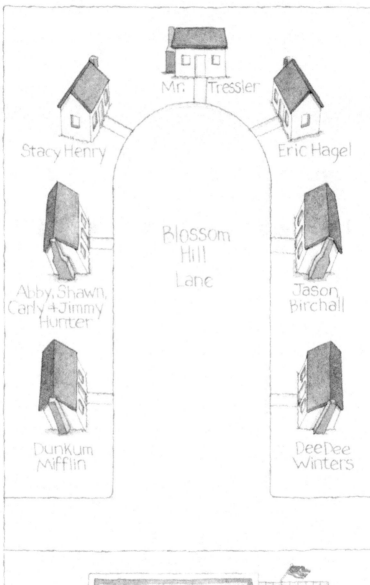

ONE

It was five days before Christmas break.

Eric Hagel shoved his feet into his snow boots. He peeked out his bedroom window. A full moon made the snow twinkle. He shivered thinking about his paper route.

Downstairs, Eric stuffed newspapers into his canvas bag. He wrapped his scarf around his neck and zipped up his fleece jacket. Pushing his earmuffs on, Eric stepped out into the cold morning.

Then he saw it—a moving van parked in front of the empty house next door. Snow was stuck to its huge tires.

Eric peeked around the porch. *What a*

1

giant moving van, he thought. *There must be a bunch of kids moving in!*

Ducking behind the tree in his yard, Eric watched. A man with a long nose and a pointy chin shouted orders to the movers. He waved his cane in the cold air, like someone directing traffic.

Eric dashed through the snow. He slid behind a hedge close to the garage. Now he could see better.

He watched as the man's long coat billowed out like a cape.

"Put the boxes in the living room," the man said. His voice sounded gruff. And a little scary.

Eric glanced at his watch . . . 6:30. Plenty of time before school started.

The movers carried in a sofa and chair. And beds and lamps and boxes. Eric kept waiting for some kids to show up. Surely the new neighbor didn't live by himself. Surely he had a family . . . or someone.

A gust of wind blew Eric's green scarf across his eyes. He pushed it back quickly.

The old man paced back and forth. Then he stopped. He was staring at the hedge. Could he see Eric hiding behind it?

Quickly, Eric stuffed his scarf inside his coat. He pushed his newspaper bag down. He could feel his heart thumping.

The old man shuffled to the edge of the sidewalk.

Eric shivered.

Then the old man mumbled something, but Eric couldn't understand it.

Maybe he was having a bad day. Moving was like that sometimes.

Eric remembered the day he moved to Blossom Hill Lane. It was no fun. Not till he met the Cul-de-sac Kids. Now, there was no better place on earth!

We stick together, no matter what, Abby Hunter had always said. And it was true from the first time he met them. The Cul-de-sac Kids were true friends.

4

Eric decided he would be the one to welcome the new kids. The ones he hoped were
moving into the house at the end of Blossom
Hill Lane. He would do it—even if he had
to spy a little first.

TWO

Eric watched the old man go inside. He wanted to ask where his family was. But it was time to deliver papers.

Eric got up and brushed the snow off his knees. He crossed the street to Stacy Henry's house. A light was on in the kitchen. Stacy's mother was probably getting her crockpot ready. She worked long hours.

Eric opened the storm door. He tried not to shake the Christmas wreath. Then he put the newspaper inside.

Abby Hunter's house, next door, was dark except for Christmas lights. Around each window, red, white and green lights flashed on and off. On and off.

Next came Dunkum's house. His real name was Edward Mifflin, but nobody called him that. He was Dunkum, the hottest third grade basketball player around.

Eric opened the storm door. He placed the newspaper inside.

Eric did the same thing at each house. He wanted to keep the papers dry for the customers.

Someone was up early at Dee Dee Winter's house. Probably her dad. Mr. Winters had a long drive to work in the mountains.

Eric turned left at the end of the cul-de-sac. He had a bunch more houses to go.

The sky was turning grayish pink. It would be dawn soon.

★ ★ ★

At last, Eric headed home. His mother's hot blueberry oatmeal was waiting.

In the corner of the kitchen, his grandpa's birds chirped their morning song. Three canaries and a pair of parakeets.

Soon, Eric heard Abby Hunter's whistle. The Cul-de-sac Kids were heading for Blossom Hill School.

Eric's mother hugged him. Then he pulled on his boots, jacket and scarf. Again.

He dashed out the front door, letting it slam.

Across the street, Abby and her new Korean brothers, Shawn and Jimmy, packed clumps of snow into balls.

Stacy Henry hid behind her snowman. She laughed as the snowballs flew at her.

Dee Dee Winters was halfway down the cul-de-sac, skipping through piles of snow. She strapped on her red backpack. It was probably filled with Christmas cookies for her teacher. Dee Dee was the best first grade cookie-maker ever.

Carly Hunter, Abby's little sister, followed

Dee Dee. They were best friends. They giggled and kicked the snow in the street.

Dunkum and Jason Birchall raced and slid. They zoomed up and down Dunkum's driveway. After school they would go sledding down Blossom Hill—mean and steep—three blocks away. Eric, too.

Eric hurried to catch up. His pants stuck to his knees. It was from kneeling in the snow, spying on the new neighbor. "Wait up!" he called to Dunkum and Jason.

Abby ran up to him. "What took you so long today?"

Eric pointed to the house with the moving van. "I wanted to see who was moving in."

Stacy tossed a snowball to Abby. Abby caught it and threw it back.

"Were you spying, Eric?" Stacy asked, grinning.

"Just welcoming the new neighbors," Eric said, grinning.

"There's only one," said Stacy.

Eric pulled at his wet jeans. "Who says?"

"Abby does," Stacy insisted.

"You sure there are no kids?" Eric said.

Stacy nodded. "Right now, Shawn and Jimmy are the newest kids on the block." She chased Abby's brothers. They were too fast for her.

Eric tramped through the deepest snow he could find. He grumbled under his breath. "I hope they're wrong," he whispered. "Who wants to live all alone?"

Eric felt sorry for the old man. He remembered when he and his mother were alone. It was after his father died in Germany. Then his mother invited Grandpa to live with them. That's when they came to America.

That was two years ago—when Eric was in first grade.

Eric turned around and looked down the cul-de-sac. Just as he did, the man with the pointy chin stood in the window of his house. He was leaning on his cane. He seemed to be looking right at Eric.

Eric froze in place.

11

The man *was* looking at him!

Eric shivered. His stomach flip-flopped.

Then the curtains closed.

Eric turned around. He ran to catch up with his friends. But all he could think of was the man at the end of the cul-de-sac. *Why is he alone? Is he as creepy as he looks?*

The bell rang as Eric started across the schoolyard. "Wait for me!" he called.

"Hurry up," shouted Dunkum. "We'll be late!"

The school bell rang.

Eric slid down the sidewalk and hurried into the school.

THREE

Eric pounded down the hall toward the third grade. He pushed the door open. Miss Hershey was writing on the board.

Eric pulled his boots off and hung up his jacket. Then he slid into his seat behind Dunkum. He tapped his friend on the shoulder.

Dunkum turned around. "What?"

"There's an old man at the end of the block. And he's uh, real scary," Eric whispered.

Dunkum frowned. "There is?"

Eric described the old man's long dark coat, the cane, his face and . . .

"Eric Hagel," Miss Hershey said.

Eric looked up. "I'm here."

13

Miss Hershey was calling roll. Eric would have to tell Dunkum the rest of the story at recess.

Abby was passing back the spelling tests from last week. Eric made a 100. Yes!

He leaned up to look at Dunkum's. But Dunkum put his hand over the grade at the top of his paper.

Too late, Eric saw it.

"Don't worry," Eric said. "I'll help you drill for the next test."

Dunkum picked at the eraser on his pencil. "OK," he muttered.

Eric looked at the new spelling list. The words were: *Yule, candlelight, carols, wreath, tinsel, holly, angels,* and *mystery.*

Mystery? Eric stared at the word. What was it doing on the Christmas spelling list?

Squeezing his pencil, Eric began to write the words in his best cursive.

It wasn't easy. Eric kept seeing the old man's face. It showed up when he wrote the

14

date in the lefthand corner. It appeared when he wrote his name on the right side.

Eric rubbed his eyes. He had to get the man's face out of his mind!

He looked at the flag. He counted to ten under his breath. Then he looked at Miss Hershey. Her bright red and green Christmas sweater might help him forget the scary face.

"Eric, are you all right?" Miss Hershey asked.

He nodded. Everything would be all right soon, he told himself.

★   ★   ★

After school, Eric went sledding down Blossom hill with Dunkum and Jason. Eric forgot about the scary face. It was almost dark when the boys headed home.

"Are you still gonna help me with my spelling?" Dunkum asked Eric.

"Sure am," Eric said. "But I have to get

home after that and finish my book report."

"What's your book about?" Jason asked.

"It's a mystery," Eric answered.

"Sounds good," Jason said. "I like mysteries."

Dunkum's sled got stuck in the snow. He pulled hard on the rope. "Mysteries are OK, I guess."

Jason laughed. "The scarier the better."

"Don't they give you bad dreams?" asked Dunkum.

"Sometimes," Jason said. "But if I pray before I go to bed, it's better."

Eric pulled his scarf tighter. "Why don't you just skip the scary stuff?"

Dunkum said, "Yeah, remember that Bible verse about only thinkin' on good stuff?"

"The Bible says that?" Eric said.

Dunkum smiled. "I learned it when I first went to Abby's church. You should come see the Christmas program. I'm gonna be Joseph this year."

17

"Who's Mary?" Jason asked.

"Abby Hunter," Dunkum said. His cheeks turned red. But not just from the cold.

Eric scooped up some snow and licked it.

FOUR

Eric pulled his sled toward his house. Before going inside, he glanced next door.

The moving van was gone, and the garage door was closed. Everything looked dark . . . till someone lit a candle in the living room. And another and another. Soon the room was filled with a spooky glow.

What was going on? Didn't the old man have electricity?

I saw lights this morning, Eric thought.

Leaving his sled on the porch, Eric kicked his boots off inside the front door. He smelled German sausage. Yum!

Eric's mother was setting the dining room table. Grandpa was talking to his birds.

Eric went to the kitchen to wash his hands. They were frosty from sledding.

His mother came into the kitchen. "I've been thinking about inviting Mr. Tressler for supper sometime."

Grandpa turned away from the bird cages. "Who?"

"Our new neighbor," Mrs. Hagel said.

"Very thoughtful," said Grandpa. "I'd like to meet the old fellow."

Eric dried his hands and hurried into the dining room. He didn't know what to say. How could he tell his mother he was scared of Mr. Tressler?

Eric's mother brought in the steaming sausage, and potato salad mixed with caraway seeds.

Eric's grandfather chuckled. "I think those birds want a taste of sausage."

Eric pulled his chair out and sat down. Grandpa was bird-crazy.

"Give them some caraway seeds instead," Eric suggested.

★ ★ ★

Before dessert, Eric's mother brought out a handful of candles. She lit all of them. The dining room glowed with a magical, golden light.

Eric stared at the candles. There were twelve. They reminded him of the light in Mr. Tressler's spooky living room.

"Only twelve days till Christmas," Eric's mother said. "I hope to finish my shopping this weekend."

Eric glanced at the candle in front of his plate. He hadn't even started shopping. Oh well, there was plenty of time left.

He daydreamed into the candlelight. Suddenly, the old man's face popped out! It was the same scary face he'd seen that morning.

Yikes! Eric rubbed his eyes.

"Are you tired?" his mother asked.

"No," Eric said quickly. He didn't want to be sent off to bed early. That would spoil his plans. The plans to spy on the mystery man.

FIVE

After supper, Eric hurried to Dunkum's house. The Christmas spelling list was ready.

Eric gave the first word. "Spell yule."

Dunkum tried and missed. He left the "e" off the end. "I don't get it," he said.

Eric held up a dictionary. "Find it in here."

Dunkum looked and looked. At last he said, "Here it is. It means you will. You will shouldn't be on a Christmas spelling list."

"Not y-o-u'-l-l," Eric said. "Yule is a Christmas word. Here, let me show you." He found the word in the dictionary. Y-u-l-e. Eric let Dunkum read it.

"Yule means Christmas?" asked Dunkum.

23

Eric nodded. "In Germany, where I was born, people used to burn yule logs at Christmas. It's a giant piece of firewood. Sometimes the whole trunk of a tree."

"Wow! The whole trunk?" said Dunkum.

"Yep."

"How does it fit into the fireplace?" asked Dunkum.

"Our fireplaces can't hold a yule log, but in the old days they could. Now my mom lights candles instead."

Eric looked at the next word on the list. *Candlelight*. "I'll give you a hint," he said. "This word is two words put together. It's a compound word."

First try, Dunkum spelled it right.

Eric drilled his friend on all the words. When they came to *mystery*, Eric scratched his head. "I wonder why Miss Hershey put this word on the list."

"Maybe she knows about the first Christmas," Dunkum replied.

"What do you mean?" Eric asked.

"Well, the first Christmas was a true mystery. Only God could have set it up."

Eric closed the dictionary. "Huh?"

"For one thing, Joseph and Mary didn't live in Bethlehem. But God knew way ahead of time that Jesus was gonna be born there." Dunkum sat down beside Eric on the floor.

"What else?" Eric said.

"Jesus was God's son—but he was also a man. That's a good mystery for you," said Dunkum.

"Yeah," said Eric. "You're right."

"That's not all," said Dunkum. "The first Christmas was about presents—the best one of all. A baby boy named Jesus."

"Sounds like you really got this stuff down," Eric said.

"I learned it at church," Dunkum said.

Eric thought about the spelling list. "Does Miss Hershey go, too?" he asked.

Dunkum stood up. "I've never seen her there. But I have a feeling she goes to church somewhere."

It was time to leave. Eric had important plans. He headed straight for Mr. Tressler's house. The moon was as big as a basketball. Full moons were like that.

Just then, Dee Dee's kitten jumped out of the bushes. Eric stopped. A cat this small could freeze to death. Eric ran after him. "Come here, Mister Whiskers."

Meow. The cat headed down the sidewalk to Mr. Tressler's. Leaping over mounds of snow, Mister Whiskers seemed to know where he was going. Straight to the old man's front porch!

Eric's heart was pounding hard. "Here, kitty, kitty," he called softly. Eric tiptoed through the snow, reaching out for the fluffy gray kitten.

Then Mister Whiskers leaped onto the window sill. Boldly, he pranced across.

This is horrible! thought Eric. Then he looked up.

He could see the old man's shadow in the

window. By the light of a dozen candles, Mr. Tressler was putting up a Christmas tree.

Eric couldn't see clearly through the sheer curtain. But he could see Mr. Tressler's long nose and pointy chin.

Eric shivered in the darkness. The whole thing was creepy. He moved closer to get a better look.

Candles flickered in the window. Moon shadows danced on the snow. Then Mister Whiskers meowed like a trumpet in the stillness.

"Be quiet!" Eric shouted.

FLASH—the porch light.

Eric spun around and ran for his life!

SIX

Eric slammed his front door. He leaned hard against it, gasping for breath. He was safe!

"What's the matter?" his mother asked.

Eric tossed his jacket onto the hook in the closet. His chest moved up and down. He could hardly talk.

"Eric, are you all right?" she said.

He waved his hands in front of his face. "It's Mister Whiskers . . . he's out there . . . in the cold . . . somewhere."

"That poor little thing?"

Eric nodded. "I was trying to catch him

29

and take him home." It was only half the truth.

"Well, I think you'd better bundle up and try again." She pulled his coat down off the hook and held it up.

Eric didn't say a word. He was too scared. Too scared to go back out there and look for Mister Whiskers. Closing the door behind him, Eric stayed on his front porch. It felt safer there.

He looked at Mr. Tressler's house. The porch light was still on. But Mister Whiskers was nowhere to be seen.

Slowly, Eric crept into the night.

He studied the shadows behind the living room curtains. It looked like Mr. Tressler was decorating his tree.

If only he had Grandpa's field glasses. His grandpa used them for bird-watching in the spring. Eric wished he had them now. He could stay far enough away from the old man's house.

30

Eric went back inside. He asked Grandpa for the field glasses—very politely.

"Why do you want them?" Grandpa asked.

"They might help me find Mister Whiskers." Eric felt bad about lying to Grandpa.

"How can you find a cat in the dark?" his grandfather asked.

"Please, just let me try?" Eric pleaded.

Grandpa pulled himself up out of his chair. He muttered something and went upstairs.

Eric crossed his fingers, hoping.

When his grandpa came down, Eric saw the field glasses. Yes!

Promising to take care of them, Eric dashed outside. Now . . . for a good hiding place.

He looked around the cul-de-sac. His eyes stopped in front of Stacy's house. There stood her fat snowman. It was perfect!

He crossed the street and headed for the snowman.

Crouching down, Eric held the glasses. He turned the button. Slowly, Mr. Tressler's living room came into view. Candles flickered everywhere.

Through the curtains, Eric saw Mr. Tressler hang a string of Christmas lights. He wondered if the old man was smiling. He wished he could see his face. Eric remembered the scary face and changed his mind.

Mr. Tressler hung up some round ornaments. Last, the Christmas angel.

Eric could almost hear Mr. Tressler grunting and groaning as he reached up. Just like Grandpa. The angel came to rest at the top. The old man stepped back for a long look.

Then the most shocking thing happened. Mr. Tressler stepped closer to the tree. He reached up to touch the angel and . . .

It began to fly! Around and around the room it glided.

Eric felt glued to the spot behind the snowman. Reading about stuff like this was one thing. But seeing it? Wait till he told the Cul-de-sac Kids!

He stood on his toes for a better look. The

angel was still doing its thing. Drifting through the air, around the living room!

"Whatcha doin'?" someone said behind him.

Eric jumped a foot high.

It was Dee Dee Winters.

"You should *never* sneak up behind someone like that!" Eric scolded.

"Mister Whiskers is lost!"

"I know. I'll help you in a second," Eric said. "Here, look through these first." He held the field glasses up for Dee Dee. "See that angel flying around?"

Dee Dee was silent as she watched. Little puffs of air came out of her nose. Finally, she said, "Wow! What's happenin' over there?"

"Crazy, isn't it?" Eric said.

Dee Dee nodded. Her eyes grew bigger and bigger. "I've never seen a real angel before."

"Me neither."

Dee Dee was shivering hard.

"Come on, I'll help you find your cat," Eric said.

They crossed the street together.

Meow. Meow.

Eric stopped. "Did you hear that?"

Dee Dee called, "Here, Mister Whiskers."

More meows. Shaky, shivery meows.

They found frosty Mister Whiskers under Eric's porch. Dee Dee bent down and picked him up. "Thank you, Eric."

"It was nothing," he said. "Hurry home. And be careful who you talk to—about Mr. Tressler's angel."

"I'm gonna call Carly right away." And she turned around and left.

Eric darted into his house. He had to make some phone calls, too.

The crazy Christmas angel was stranger than any mystery he had ever read!

SEVEN

Eric called Dunkum first. "You'll never believe what I saw tonight," he bragged.

Dunkum was all ears. He wanted to see for himself. Abby and Jason and Stacy did too.

So . . . Eric had a plan. The Cul-de-sac Kids would have a meeting tomorrow night— behind the snowman in Stacy's yard.

Terrific!

He zipped off to his room to do his homework. The book report was due tomorrow. He would have to write fast to get it done.

Knock, knock.

"Come in," Eric called.

It was Grandpa. He wanted his field glasses back.

Gulp! Eric scratched his head. He must have left them outside. His face was getting hot. It was his own fault. His, and that crazy angel's!

"Wait, Grandpa. I'll be right back," Eric said. He flew down the stairs, yanked at his coat, and ran outside.

Eric scrambled across the street to the snowman. He leaned over to look. Nothing.

He got down on his hands and knees. He patted the snowy ground. Nothing.

Grandpa's field glasses were gone!

Eric felt the lump in his throat grow bigger. He stood up and leaned against the snowman. He brushed the snow off his jeans.

When he looked up, the field glasses were staring at him. Carefully, he picked them off the snowman's shoulder.

Eric held them up and looked through them.

Whew! They were okay.

While he was checking them, something caught his eye. Across the street, at Mr. Tressler's house things were crazy. Crazier than ever!

Eric tuned up the field glasses. Could it be true? Were his eyes playing tricks?

Slowly, Eric moved towards Mr. Tressler's house. He got as close as the hedge.

Field glasses do not lie.

The angels had multiplied! Dozens were flying around the old man. He was swaying this way and that way. Mr. Tressler was dancing with the angels. It looked like he was having the time of his life.

Eric wanted to watch forever. Something deep inside him sprang up. It was a strange, warm feeling and it wouldn't go away. He knew he had to meet Mr. Tressler. Face-to-face!

Eric rushed to the old man's front porch. He shook as he stuffed the field glasses into his pocket. More than anything, he wanted to ring the doorbell. But his finger wouldn't move. He forced his arm up—shaking with fear.

"Eric!" It was Grandpa's voice.

Eric jumped a foot. The second time tonight. He leaped over the snowy walkway to his house. He held up the field glasses. "Here they are, Grandpa."

Grandpa frowned.

"I'm sorry about your glasses," Eric said. He was sorry about something else, too. Not getting to meet Mr. Tressler.

"Those glasses were expensive," Grandpa said, shaking his finger at Eric.

Eric looked up at Grandpa's soft blue eyes. "It won't happen again. I promise."

"And that is the truth," Grandpa muttered. He climbed the stairs, grunting all the way.

So much for borrowing Grandpa's stuff. Eric dashed upstairs to finish his book report.

Then he thought of something. If he hadn't left Grandpa's glasses outside, he might have missed the strange sight next door. The angels had multiplied!

Now Eric had a big mystery on his hands. And he didn't know what to do about it.

Then he had an idea. It might not solve the mystery, but it would show a little kindness.

EIGHT

The next morning, Eric trudged through the snow. He headed to Mr. Tressler's house— to deliver a newspaper free of charge. Eric would pay for it himself, out of his earnings.

Eric tiptoed up the porch steps. He turned the handle on the storm door. And he placed the paper in the space between two doors.

Inside, a cuckoo clock sang out the time. Six cuckoos in a row.

Eric checked his watch. Six o'clock, right on the dot. He turned to leave, but the sound of a flute stopped him. It was coming from inside Mr. Tressler's house.

Eric froze in his tracks.

Mr. Tressler plays the flute.

Eric listened.

It was music for the angels! He chuckled to himself as silver full-moon sounds floated around him.

He leaned against the porch railing and felt lucky—the only one to hear the magic. He breathed it in and held it close.

Then the music stopped. And the front door opened. Eric sprang off the porch and dashed down the street.

★   ★   ★

After supper, the Cul-de-sac Kids met in Stacy's front yard as planned. Abby was president, so she called the meeting to order. That was easy. The only reason for the meeting was to see the angels. At Mr. Tressler's house.

Dunkum set up his telescope. Eric had first look. The angels were flying all right. And Mr. Tressler was prancing and swaying.

42

Carly and Dee Dee took turns looking through the telescope. Shawn and Jimmy were next.

Jason couldn't wait his turn. "If there's a man dancing with angels, I've got to see it!" He walked across the street for a closer look. Dunkum followed.

Eric stayed behind with Abby and Stacy, near the snowman.

"I should invite Mr. Tressler to our Christmas play," Abby said. "He could appear to the shepherds and bring his heavenly host."

Stacy laughed. "Good idea."

"What do you think makes them fly, Eric?" Abby said, after her turn.

"Batteries, probably," said Eric. But he didn't know. Not really. He watched as the angels circled Mr. Tressler's head.

Carly asked, "Do the batteries ever run down?"

"Sooner or later," Eric said, like he knew.

Just then, Dunkum and Jason came running. "Huddle up," Dunkum called.

44

The kids grabbed each other's arms and made a circle.

Dunkum had a plan. "Let's take a Christmas present to Mr. Tressler. Then we can find out what's going on in there."

"We've done enough spying," said Abby. "Let's sing Christmas carols for him. To welcome him to the cul-de-sac."

Everyone liked that idea. Everyone but Eric.

"I sing flat," Eric said.

"You could whistle," Abby suggested.

Leave it to Abby, thought Eric.

"Someone needs to introduce us after we sing," Abby said.

The kids looked at Eric.

"Why me?" Eric said.

"You got us out here," said Dunkum.

"Yeah, hurry up, it's cold," said Dee Dee.

Eric didn't want to do the talking. He didn't want to whistle Christmas carols. Besides, what if Mr. Tressler was real creepy and scared everyone away?

What then?

NINE

"It's too late to go caroling now," Eric said. He was chickening out.

Abby stuck up for him. "Eric's right—besides, we need to practice first."

"How about everyone giving Mr. Tressler a gift? I'll make him a Christmas card," Stacy said. She was good at that.

"Definitely," said Abby.

"Don't forget the Christmas cookies," Dee Dee piped up.

Shawn wanted to give something, too. "I teach Mr. Tressler Korean folk tune."

Jimmy jumped up and down. "I sing, too!"

"Hey, great idea," said Dunkum.

47

"What about you?" Eric asked him. "What will you bring?"

Dunkum laughed. "Maybe I could write a poem about angels and mysteries. You know, from the Christmas spelling list."

Eric liked that. So did the others.

Jason couldn't stand still. He was like that when his hyper medicine wore off. "I could dance with Mr. Tressler's angels," said Jason. He jigged around the snowman.

Dee Dee giggled. "Me too!"

"If we sing the carols loud enough, he might open the door," said Jason. "Then we can see those flying Christmas angels of his."

"Wait a minute," Carly spoke up. "I thought we were doing it to be friendly—*not* to spy."

Abby put her arm around her little sister. Carly grinned up at Abby in the moonlit night.

The moonlight reminded Eric of Mr. Tressler's flute. That strange, warm feeling stirred inside him again. Maybe caroling for Mr.

Tressler wasn't such a bad idea. Maybe he would give the old man a gift after all.

"I want to give our new neighbor something he'll never forget," Eric said.

"What is it?" the kids shouted.

"A friend," Eric said. He was thinking of his grandpa.

"Now everyone has something to give," said Abby. "Meet tomorrow after school at Dunkum's."

The kids scattered and went home.

Eric still wasn't sure about those angels. Did they run on batteries? Maybe not. Maybe Mr. Tressler was a true angel keeper. If so, Grandpa might be just the friend for him.

Sometimes, late at night, Eric could hear Grandpa talking to God. Some people called it praying. But with Grandpa it was just plain talking.

Eric went to his room and put on his pajamas. He thought about Mr. Tressler. How could the old man dance with angels and still be so creepy?

TEN

It was December 15th.

After school, the Cul-de-sac Kids met at Dunkum's. They practiced five songs. They sang them five times in a row. "Silent Night" and "Jingle Bells" were good, but "Angels We Have Heard on High" was the best.

Eric whistled. Jason jigged. And Abby said they sounded double dabble good.

★ ★ ★

The next night, the kids lined up on Mr. Tressler's porch. Candles burned in the window. No one moved. Eric took a deep breath and pressed the doorbell.

When the porch light came on, the kids started to sing "Joy to the World." Eric whistled along.

Slowly the door opened.

There stood the old man without a smile. He reached for his cane!

Eric froze.

Mr. Tressler raised his cane in the air.

He's gonna chase us away! thought Eric.

Instead, the cane began to wave in time to the music. Mr. Tressler kept it up through "Silent Night" and "Frosty the Snowman."

But then, Mr. Tressler left.

What should they do?

Eric started whistling "Jingle Bells" as loud as he could.

The old man came back with his flute. He began to play along, with his eyes closed.

Eric felt a lump in his throat. The old man wasn't scary. Not one bit!

At the end, the kids clapped.

Mr. Tressler bowed low. "Thank you kindly," he said. "And you—what voices! You sound like the angels."

Angels! Eric peeked around the corner. He didn't see any angels. Had the batteries run down?

Abby pointed to Eric. It was time for him to talk. He introduced Stacy Henry first.

Stacy gave Mr. Tressler an angel Christmas card made from white construction paper. Glittery gold.

"Welcome to our cul-de-sac," she said.

"Thank you, dear," said Mr. Tressler.

Eric pointed to Dee Dee Winters and said her name.

She handed him a basket of Christmas cookies. "I hope you like angel cookies."

Carly stood beside her. "She made them and I sprinkled them." The girls giggled.

The old man nodded. "Thank you, indeed."

Eric said, "Now Shawn and Jimmy Hunter want to teach you a Korean folksong."

The boys started to sing. The rest of the kids tried to join in on the chorus. Everyone clapped at the end. Even Mr. Tressler.

Dunkum seemed shy when his turn came. "I made up a poem for you."

Eric could see the words *angel* and *mystery* on the paper. They were spelled right. Good for Dunkum!

Abby Hunter smiled when Eric introduced her. "I have a gift for you, but you must come to my church on Christmas Eve to get it. It's the Christmas play. I'm going to be Mary."

Mr. Tressler smiled for the first time. "Why thank you, I'd be delighted."

Jason Birchall was next. He couldn't stand still. "Want a fast dance or a slow one?" he asked.

"As you wish," Mr. Tressler said.

Jason began his jig. It looked like he was making it up as he went.

Then Mr. Tressler began to play his flute. It was "Jingle Bells" with lots of extra notes.

Jason's jig got better and better.

At the end, Mr. Tressler said, "Now I have a surprise for all of you."

Eric peeked through the storm door. He could see Mr. Tressler heading for the kitchen. But he didn't see any angels.

What was going on?

ELEVEN

Eric heard a soft cooing sound.

Mr. Tressler was coming through the living room. Eric leaned forward to see.

What was that on his shoulders?

Eric couldn't help it. He stared.

Mr. Tressler stood in the doorway. He was covered with white doves! They perched on his shoulders. And on his head. When he cupped his hands, three flew into them.

So these are the angels! thought Eric.

The birds seemed so comfortable around the old man. It was like he was their trusted friend.

Dee Dee's eyes grew wide.

Carly giggled.

Abby's jaw dropped two feet.

Stacy whispered, "Wow!"

Dunkum scratched his head and stared.

Shawn and Jimmy watched silently.

Jason blinked his eyes faster than ever.

Softly, Mr. Tressler began to whistle. The doves cooed along. Eric could see their short legs under their round bodies. What a strange sight.

Doves do look like tiny angels, thought Eric. *All in white with big wings.*

Eric felt good inside. Mr. Tressler wasn't like anyone he'd ever met. Except maybe for Grandpa.

Grandpa loved birds, that was no secret. And sometimes he did strange things, too. Like tramping around in the spring, spying on birds with his field glasses.

Mr. Tressler stopped whistling. "Merry Christmas, kids," he said, waving his arms. The doves flew to the Christmas tree. They perched on the branches.

The kids shouted, "Merry Christmas Mr. Tressler!"

The new neighbor wore the widest grin on Blossom Hill Lane.

Eric whispered to him, "You whistle good."

The old man winked at him. "So do you."

"Want to come caroling, uh, whistling with us?" Eric asked.

Mr. Tressler reached for his cane. And his long brown coat. It looked just fine. Not creepy at all.

First stop, Eric's house.

Eric pressed the doorbell. He stood beside Mr. Tressler. They whistled while the others sang "Silent Night." They sounded good.

Grandpa came to the door. Eric introduced him to Mr. Tressler. Grandpa gave Eric a big hug, then he grabbed his coat and hat. He joined the group as they caroled around the cul-de-sac.

Eric was so happy he stopped whistling and tried to sing. It sounded flat, but it didn't matter. Mr. Tressler would never have to be alone again. The Cul-de-sac Kids could be the old man's family!

Mr. Tressler's cane danced in the air as the carolers went from house to house.

Soon, they were back at the old man's house. He invited Eric's grandfather inside for coffee.

The Cul-de-sac Kids waved goodbye to them. "Merry Christmas!" they shouted.

"And a Merry Christmas to all of you," Mr. Tressler said, waving his cane. He was out of breath, but a smile burst across his long face.

Before the two men reached the porch, Eric was whistling again. It was time for his favorite carol—"Angels We Have Heard on High."

THE CUL-DE-SAC KIDS SERIES

Don't miss #4!

NO GROWN-UPS ALLOWED!

Jason Birchall can't wait for Valentine's Day! His parents are going away for the weekend and Grandma is coming! Jason has big plans! Can he trick his grandmother into allowing him to change his bedtime? Or his eating habits?

Strange things happen when Jason pigs out on chocolate and stays up late for a scary show!

Also by Beverly Lewis

Adult Nonfiction

Amish Prayers
The Beverly Lewis Amish Heritage Cookbook

Adult Fiction

HOME TO HICKORY HOLLOW

The Fiddler • The Bridesmaid • The Guardian • The Secret Keeper • The Last Bride

SEASONS OF GRACE

The Secret • The Missing • The Telling

ABRAM'S DAUGHTERS

The Covenant • The Betrayal • The Sacrifice • The Prodigal • The Revelation

ANNIE'S PEOPLE

The Preacher's Daughter • The Englisher • The Brethren

THE ROSE TRILOGY

The Thorn • The Judgment • The Mercy

THE COURTSHIP OF NELLIE FISHER

The Parting • The Forbidden • The Longing

THE HERITAGE OF LANCASTER COUNTY

The Shunning • The Confession • The Reckoning

OTHER ADULT FICTION

The Postcard • The Crossroad • The Redemption of Sarah Cain
October Song • Sanctuary* • The Sunroom • Child of Mine*
The River • The Love Letters • The Photograph

Youth Fiction

Girls Only (GO!) Volume One and *Volume Two*[†]
SummerHill Secrets Volume One and *Volume Two*[‡]
Holly's Heart Collection One[†], *Collection Two*[‡], and *Collection Three*[†]

www.BeverlyLewis.com

* with David Lewis [†] 4 books in each volume [‡] 5 books in each volume

ABOUT THE AUTHOR

Beverly Lewis plays Christmas music in August. In December she helps her kids make Snow Creatures. Dressing them up in "people" clothes is giggle-time.

Beverly's never seen a flying angel. But she has heard the silvery full-moon sound of a flute, played by her sister, Barbara Birch—who designs the pictures in these books.

Other chapter books you'll enjoy by Beverly: MOUNTAIN BIKES AND GARBANZO BEANS and THE SIX-HOUR MYSTERY.

(ages 7–10)

AstroKids™
by Robert Elmer

Space scooters? Floating robots? Jupiter ice cream? Blast into the future for out-of-this-world, zero-gravity fun with the AstroKids on space station *CLEO-7*.

The Cul-de-sac Kids
by Beverly Lewis

Each story in this lighthearted series features the hilarious antics and predicaments of nine endearing boys and girls who live on Blossom Hill Lane.

Janette Oke's Animal Friends
by Janette Oke

Endearing creatures from the farm, forest, and zoo discover their place in God's world through various struggles, mishaps, and adventures.

Made in the USA
Monee, IL
11 November 2022

17581275R00049